This book belongs to

....

How this collection works

This collection of traditional tales offers four well-loved stories from around the world for you and your child to enjoy together: *Lots of Nuts, Run, Run!, The Big Carrot* and *Get the Rat!* They are based on traditional stories that your child may already be familiar with, but have been written so that your child can read them for themselves. They are carefully levelled and in line with your child's phonics learning at school. In addition, each story is accompanied by an optional extended story text for parents to read aloud to their child, to offer the richness that the original story language provides.

How to use this book

Find a time to read with your child when they are happy to concentrate for about 5–10 minutes. Reading with your child should be a shared and enjoyable experience. Choose one or two stories for each session, so they don't get too tired.

Please read the tips on the next page of this collection, as they offer suggestions and ideas for how to get the most out of this story collection.

Enjoy sharing the stories!

Tips for reading the stories together

Step 1 – Before you begin, ask your child to read the title of the story. Talk about what the story might be about. To set the scene of the story, read the extended story text available before each story. This will provide the rich story language of the original story and will familiarise the child with the plot and the characters before they read the story for themselves. Talk about the story and what your child liked and didn't like.

Step 2 – Now encourage your child to read the illustrated story to you. Talk about the pictures as you read. Your child will be able to read most of the words in the story, but if they struggle with a word, remind them to say the sounds in the word from left to right and then blend the sounds together to read the whole word, e.g. n-u-t-s, nuts. If they come across a tricky word that they cannot sound out, simply read the word to the child, e.g. the, I, go.

Step 3 – After you have read the story, talk about what happened. How are all the different characters feeling at the end of the story? Encourage your child to use the story map that follows each story to retell the story to you in their own words. It's a fun way of helping them to understand the story and to learn to tell stories in their own way.

Contents

OXFORD
UNIVERSITY PRESS

Lots of Nuts

Long ago and far away, a little mouse lived in a wood. He was a country mouse, as thin as a rail, and his name was Tim.

One day, as he was eating his breakfast of crunchy munchy nuts, another mouse strolled into the wood. He was a town mouse, as fat as butter, and his name was Tom. Tom tipped up his smart little hat, tapped his cane, and twitched his whiskers.

"What are you eating, country mouse?" he asked.

"A nut!" replied Tim. "I eat lots of delicious nuts – whatever I can find in the wood. Why don't you try one?"

Tom popped a nut into his mouth. And then he spat it straight out again!

"Huff! I don't like nuts! I'm going back to my house in the town. Back to my cream buns and trifles! Why don't you come with me, country mouse?"

Well, Tim thought he would like to see the town, and to taste those delicious dishes. So the two mice ran across the fields, up hills and down dales, to the house. In the kitchen, they had a wonderful feast! Cream buns, cakes and pastries, trifles and jellies, fruit and cheese ...

"I like being a town mouse!" thought Tim, his mouth full of squishy squashy cream bun.

Suddenly, a huge dog burst into the kitchen, growling and barking. Tim could see his sharp white teeth and his long wet tongue.

"Ruff! Ruff! There's a stranger in the house!" barked the dog.

Tim was so frightened that he dropped his bun!

"What's the matter, country mouse?" asked Tom. "It's only a dog! In the town, people need guard dogs to keep robbers away."

But Tim didn't stop to hear more. Oh, no, indeed! All he could think of was his cosy house in the wood, and his pile of nuts.

He ran across fields, he ran up hills and down dales, until at last he was back in the wood. And there, with all his woodland friends looking on, he had a *truly* wonderful feast – lots of nuts!

Tim said, "Mmmmmmmm! Nuts are good enough for me!"

Lots of Nuts

Written by Gill Munton

Illustrated by Emma Dodson

Tim had lots
of nuts.

Tim

9

Tom had a big
bag of buns.

10

11

A big dog ran in!

Ruff, ruff!

12

Once upon a time...

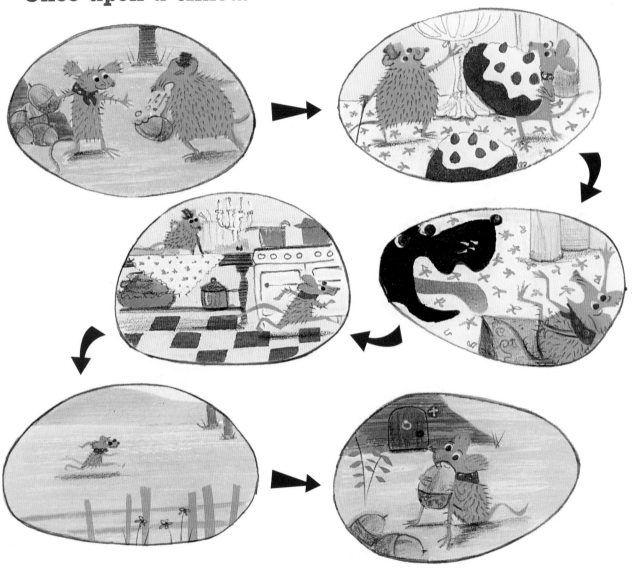

The end.

Run, Run `Extended Story`

Once upon a time, there lived a man and his wife and their cat. One fine day they baked gingerbread biscuits together and as they waited for the delicious-smelling biscuits to cool, something incredible happened …

One of the biscuits sat up, and before the man, his wife and the cat could even blink, the Gingerbread Man slipped off the baking tray, dashed across the kitchen and climbed up onto the window sill.

The astonished man and his wife tried to grab him, but the little man hopped down from the window as quick as a wink calling, "Run, run as fast as you can. You can't catch me, I'm the Gingerbread Man!"

The cat, the woman and her husband all raced out of the house and along the path after the Gingerbread Man. They ran as fast as their legs would carry them, but the Gingerbread Man ran faster.

He laughed with glee as he sprinted ahead calling, "Run, run as fast as you can. You can't catch me, I'm the Gingerbread Man!"

The family chased him over the hills and far away from home. They ran until they could run no more, and still the Gingerbread Man zipped along running further and further ahead calling, "Run, run as fast as you can. You can't catch me, I'm the Gingerbread Man!"

Finally the Gingerbread Man came to a wide, fast-flowing river and he could run no more. There, curled up on the bank, was Sly Fox.

"I cannot run any further," the Gingerbread Man sighed.

"I can help you," whispered Sly Fox. "Climb onto my back and I'll carry you across the river to the other side."

So the Gingerbread Man hopped onto Sly Fox's back and waved to the family, who stood helplessly at the river's edge. But Sly Fox had a plan. He pretended that the river was deep and told the Gingerbread Man to climb onto his head so he wouldn't get wet. And the Gingerbread Man did.

When they were almost there, Sly Fox pretended the river was deeper still! And this time he told the Gingerbread Man to climb onto his nose. The second that he did, Sly Fox flipped his head up and threw the poor Gingerbread Man into the air and down he fell – snap!

And with that snap the Gingerbread Man was eaten up.

Run, Run!

Written by Alex Lane

Illustrated by Paula Metcalf

23

The cat ran.

Mum ran.

Get him!

Dad ran.

29

Once upon a time...

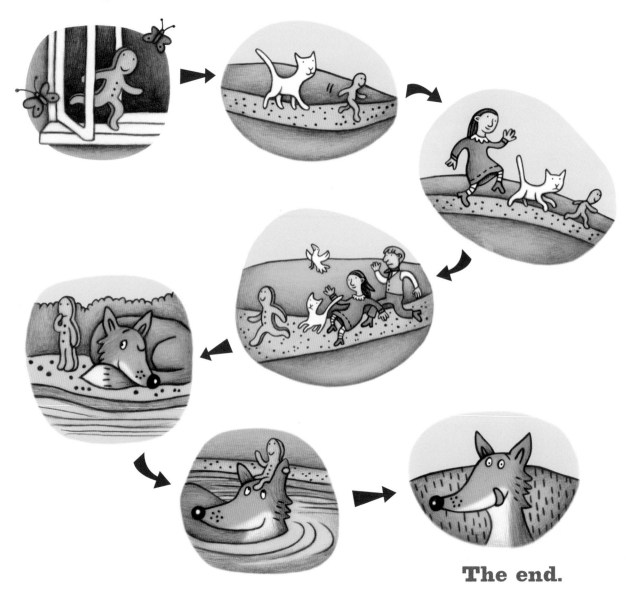

The end.

The Big Carrot

Once upon a time, a little old man grew an enormous carrot in his garden. It was just right for making into soup. He pulled and he tugged. He tugged and he pulled.

Pull! Tug! Pull! Tug!

But the carrot wouldn't budge. It was far too big for him to pull up by himself.

So a little old woman ran to help him, and together the two of them pulled and the two of them tugged. They tugged and they pulled. They pulled and they tugged!

Pull! Tug! Pull! Tug!

But the carrot just wouldn't budge!

So a little boy ran to help them, and together the three of them pulled and the three of them tugged. They tugged and they pulled. They pulled and they tugged!

Pull! Tug! Pull! Tug!

But still, the carrot just wouldn't budge!

So a little girl ran to help them, and together the four of them pulled and the four of them tugged. They tugged and they pulled. They pulled and they tugged!

Pull! Tug! Pull! Tug!

But still the carrot just wouldn't budge!

So a little dog ran to help them, and together the five of them pulled and the five of them tugged. They tugged and they pulled. They pulled and they tugged!

Pull! Tug! Pull! Tug!

But still, the carrot just wouldn't budge!

So a little cat ran to help them, and together the six of them pulled and the six of them tugged. They tugged and they pulled. They pulled and they tugged!

Pull! Tug! Pull! Tug!

But *still,* the carrot just *wouldn't* budge!

Then a tiny, little mouse ran to help them. So the little old man, the little old woman, the little boy and the little girl, the little dog and the little cat and the tiny, little mouse pulled and they tugged.
They **tugged** and they **pulled**!
They **pulled** and they **tugged** together!

Pull! Tug! Pull! Tug!

Until, at long last, POP! The enormous carrot came out of the ground! And everyone shot backwards and fell to the ground in a big heap!

Then the little old man made a big pot of carrot soup. And when the soup was hot and tasty and just right for eating, everyone had some for tea. And it tasted delicious!

The Big Carrot

Written by Alison Hawes

Illustrated by Stuart Trotter

Can Tom get the big carrot?

Tug !

Tom and Ifra
tug the big carrot.

Tom, Ifra and Nick tug.

Tom, Ifra, Nick and Lin tug.

Tom, Ifra, Nick, Lin
and Sam tug.

Tom, Ifra,
Nick, Lin,
Sam and Kit tug.

Up pops the big carrot!

Mmmmm !

45

Once upon a time...

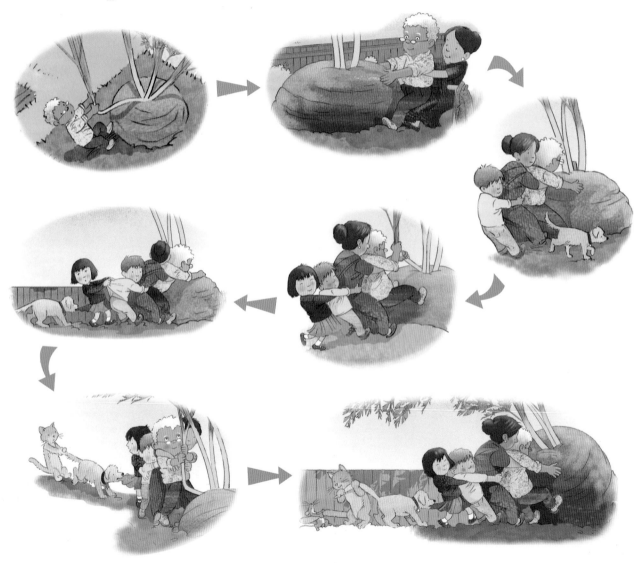

The end.

Get the Rat! Extended Story

It was lunchtime at the palace. The Princess, her father and her mother (the King and Queen), were all enjoying a quiet meal when all of a sudden, the Princess spotted something twitching, close to the royal cheese. The twitch twitched again and then she saw ... whiskers, a black twitching nose, and a long brown snaking tail!

The Princess gave a shrill shriek of fear. She pointed and screamed, "Rat! A rat is eating the royal cheese!"

Nearby, the royal cat heard the word 'rat' and woke up. It moved with lightning speed and jumped up onto the royal table to catch the fierce rat. The cat yowled past the Queen and sent the plates and dishes flying to the floor.

The Queen grabbed the hissing cat and the Princess grabbed the rat. But she looked down only to find ... a sock in her hand instead!

Meanwhile, the King called the royal footman to help catch the rat. At that exact moment, the Princess saw a dark shape in the royal teacup.

"A rat!" she shrieked. "It is in the cup!"

The footman rushed forward to grab at the tricky rat. But he fell, and sent the table flying to the floor.

The footman snatched at the fleeing rat. He looked down only to find ... a teabag in his hand instead! The Queen called the royal guards to help catch the rat. At that very instant, the Princess saw a strange furry shape in the King's crown.

"It is on his hat!" she yelled.

"Get the rat!" they shrieked.

The guards raced to the King to catch that terrible rat. But they sent the King flying and they all tumbled on to the floor in a heap.

"I have the rat!" the Queen shouted.

When the dust settled, the Queen looked down at her hand only to find ... the King's wig in her hand instead!

Everyone was exhausted and the palace was a huge mess. Unseen by anyone, the tired rat scuttled across the floor and shot out of the window.

At that very moment the Princess saw a huge insect on the window. She let out a shrill shriek ...

Get the Rat!

Written by Alex Lane

Illustrated by Sholto Walker

53

Get the rat!

It is a mess.

Once upon a time...

The end.

Make up a new story!

Now have a go at making up your own story like the ones in this book. You can use the ideas here or make up your own!

1 **Who is in your story?**

2 **What happens first?**

Perhaps the Princess meets the Gingerbread Man...
or Tim meets the rat?

③ What do they do together?

Do the Princess and the Gingerbread Man have an adventure?

Does the rat try to steal Tim's bun?

④ How will the story end?

Are the Princess and Gingerbread Man friends forever?

Do Tim and the rat find a big pile of food to share?

OXFORD
UNIVERSITY PRESS

Great Clarendon Street, Oxford, OX2 6DP, United Kingdom

Oxford University Press is a department of the University
of Oxford. It furthers the University's objective of excellence
in research, scholarship, and education by publishing worldwide.
Oxford is a registered trade mark of Oxford University Press
in the UK and in certain other countries

Text © Oxford University Press 2011

Lots of Nuts Illustrations © Emma Dodson 2011
Run, Run! Illustrations © Paula Metcalf 2011
The Big Carrot Illustrations © Stuart Trotter 2011
Get the Rat! Illustrations © Sholto Walker 2011

Extended Story text for *Lots of Nuts* written by Gill Munton
Extended Story text for *Run, Run!* written by Charlotte Raby
Extended Story text for *The Big Carrot* written by Alison Hawes
Extended story text for *Get the Rat!* written by Charlotte Raby

The moral rights of the authors have been asserted

Lots of Nuts, Run, Run!, The Big Carrot, Get the Rat! first published in 2011
This Edition published in 2018

British Library Cataloguing in Publication Data
Data available

ISBN: 978-0-19-276515-4

10 9 8 7 6 5 4 3 2

Paper used in the production of this book is a natural, recyclable
product made from wood grown in sustainable forests. The
manufacturing process conforms to the environmental
regulations of the country of origin.

Printed in China

Acknowledgements

Series Advisor: Nikki Gamble